Take one every day just before bedtime

DIRTY NOIR

DARK TALES OF LOVE, BETRAYAL, MURDER AND MORE...

MARTIN MULLIGAN

JACK D MCLEAN

Copyright (C) 2020 Jack D McLean & Martin Mulligan

Layout design and Copyright (C) 2021 by Next Chapter

Published 2021 by Next Chapter

Cover art by CoverMint

Mass Market Paperback Edition

This book is a work of fiction. Names, characters, places, and incidents are the product of the author's imagination or are used fictitiously. Any resemblance to actual events, locales, or persons, living or dead, is purely coincidental.

All rights reserved. No part of this book may be reproduced or transmitted in any form or by any means, electronic or mechanical, including photocopying, recording, or by any information storage and retrieval system, without the author's permission.

MEXICO

JACK D' MCLEAN AND MARTIN MULLIGAN

We got married in Mexico and he left me six weeks later.

I loved him, was insanely in love with him.

But you need some context for all this.

I was studying philosophy at St Edmund Hall, Oxford's oldest college, when we met, and was tipped for a first.

Adam blazed into my life and it was as if a piano had fallen on me, "with all its melodies" – that was his phrase when I shared the image with him.

He was a rally driver and engineer, and flew his own private jet, travelling regularly to French Guyana where he was supervising a comms-satellite programme for an International company with a big French government stake in it. Too many of the satellites were landing in the sea or exploding in the stratosphere. It was his job to get the programme back on track. He'd developed specialist software he claimed would revolutionise the comms-satelite industry, which he successfully used on that contract.

Good-looking, charming and successful, he had everything going for him – including me, for those mad weeks we spent together.

Then it was all over as suddenly as it'd begun. He didn't even say goodbye. Just left a note in our hotel room. I found it when I got back from a dip in the pool.

"Dear Jessica,

I've had a great time with you but I'm sorry, marriage isn't for me.

I still love you. But with the deepest regret I'm calling time on our relationship.

Please don't think badly of me.

Love,

Adam."

I shook as I read those words and rushed to the wardrobe to check if his clothes were still there. They weren't. Even his toiletries had vanished from the bathroom. When I'd established that every physical trace of him was gone I became a sobbing hysterical wreck.

When I'd recovered sufficiently to pack my suitcase, I booked a flight home and got the hotel to order me a taxi to the airport. While I was waiting in reception a middle-aged American man came up to me. He was obviously moneyed - his watch alone must've cost more than I earned in a month. The corners of his mouth were pointed towards the floor as if unable to resist the pull of gravity.

"You must be Jessica," he said.

"What if I am? What business is it of yours?" I was in no mood to socialise.

"Your husband just ran off with my wife."

He showed me a photograph of a stunning young woman at least twenty years his junior.

So, I thought to myself, Adam's note was a lie. It's not that marriage isn't for him. He found someone else and couldn't keep his dick in his pants. It's that simple.

The taxi arrived just as I was looking up from the photo of the woman my husband had run off with, sparing me the ordeal of further interaction with her aggrieved husband.

"I'm sorry, I have to go."

Picking up my bags I marched out with what little dignity I could muster.

For long enough after that I was a nervous wreck. I'd given up everything to be with Adam. The future I'd planned for myself – for both of us – had been cruelly snatched away from me.

Reality was so difficult to face that I saw a doctor who prescribed pills to help me cope. They were at their most effective when taken with copious amounts of alcohol.

Now and again I'd read a story in a newspaper about how Adam's business empire was growing, or see a photo on Instagram of him with one or another of his many stunning girlfriends. The sight of him enjoying the company of so many nubile partners was the most exquisite torture for me.

Cue more pills and drink.

In the wake of my nervous breakdown, I was unable to have a relationship for a long time. When I eventually began dating again, much to my surprise, it was a woman who stole my heart. Maybe I'd always been lesbian; or possibly it was a reaction to having been so brutally betrayed by a man.

At some point, with my new partner's help, I emerged from my alcoholic and pill-fuelled haze, picked myself up off the floor, and began to think clearly.

A simple equation formed itself in my mind: he'd taken my future away. He owed me.

I could've had a high-flying career if not for Adam. Because of him I'd abandoned my degree which would've been the key to it all, then I'd spent two years in a state of near oblivion, due to his betrayal.

It was payback time. Adam was extremely wealthy. He'd inherited a lot of money, plus he was a big earner. He could afford to compensate me for the wrongs he'd done me. Handsomely.

I saw a lawyer and instructed him to arrange my divorce and ensure I got a big payout.

It was then that I learnt how truly devious Adam had been.

Wealthy guys like him often insist on prenup agreements to protect their fortunes. He hadn't done that. Instead, he'd gotten us married in a ceremony that wasn't legally recognised anywhere but the remote Mexican village where it'd taken place.

He'd obviously been planning for the future, thinking that if someone else turned his head at some stage he could get out of our relationship as easily as he'd gotten in it.

And the cunning bastard had left me high and dry. Ruined my life.

Somehow I managed to retrain in IT and painstakingly, over a period of years, I became an internet security expert for a company based in LA, although I continued to live in the Home Counties.

It was eight years after Adam and I separated that I was in Mexico – the place held bad memories for me but that didn't stop me going – at the same time as him. I was on a business trip and he was there because, well, he was just being Adam.

I saw him but he didn't see me. I was tempted to introduce myself but I didn't. Just kept my distance. He went into a hotel and I followed discreetly, watching as he ordered a drink at the bar. I knew he'd go there. It was his favourite haunt. The place was ill-lit, thick-carpeted, marble-walled, and catered to the more vulgar of the moneyed elite. The Adams of this world.

I snuck into a dark corner. A waiter glided my way and I ordered a dry martini in a quiet voice.

Over at the bar Adam was being given his drink, a gin-and-tonic. There was a girl on a stool about a yard from him sipping an exotic cocktail. She was wearing a close-fitting white silk dress and wearing it well, her black hair cascading over honey-coloured shoulders. She looked towards Adam and gave him a shy smile. An obvious come-on.

I knew from personal and painful experience that Adam rarely hesitated when given such a smile.

He immediately instigated a conversation with the girl. They had a couple of drinks together and left. I didn't follow, assuming they'd gone for a night out, and would go to his suite later. Or maybe they'd go straight to his room.

I finished my drink and went to my own hotel.

The following evening my business trip ended so I took a flight home. After landing at Heathrow I got the express to central London and went to a room I'd hired at the Double Tree hotel. I'd been there no more than five minutes when there was a knock at the door.

"Come in," I said.

A stunning young woman entered. The girl who I'd seen Adam with in Mexico. My partner. She'd been willing to sacrifice some of her principles in order to help me. Her help had gotten me access to Adam's laptop for long enough to extract vital information about his companies and finances.

His bank accounts made for a decent immediate injection to my bank balance, via a dubious worldwide trail of transactions that would throw any investigation off the scent.

I'm selling his trade secrets via the dark web – signs are they'll fetch a very high price.

Poor old Adam. I don't think I left him with enough ready money even to pay for a flight home. He'll have to raise some cash by selling shares in his companies.

But he had better do that quickly – they'll drop in value faster than the South Sea Bubble when word gets out that all his competitors know his trade secrets.

I'm planning a holiday with my gorgeous partner. A honeymoon. We've just married in style. Maybe we'll go to Mexico and stay in an expensive hotel.

The End

THE SMALL MATTER OF A MURDER

MARTIN MULLIGAN

You don't expect to fall in love with the midget who hires you to kill her husband.

She was wearing daffodil-yellow high heels the first time we met at a Frankie & Benny's on the outskirts of a drab northern seaside resort in dead midwinter. Outside, a freezing wind howled through the empty bus station. The dark deserted promenade only half a mile away was swept clean of any human detritus by the near-gale whipping off the Irish Sea and across the beach.

She was there to brief me. I took a sip of my diet Coke and pushed a deep-fried onion ring around on my plate and listened to Jadwiga the Detonating Dwarf (her professional name) . She was a headline star of Dart's Circus. Her lovely curly haired head and strong chin were just above the level of the Formica table top in the red leather upholstered private booth in the cosy dimness of the quiet restaurant.

I could tell you about the effect her squeaky high-pitched voice had on me. Or the allure of her tiny pout. Or the way she banged the table with tears running down her cheeks as she described the hell of her domestic life. But it will be safer and simpler if I just sum up and cut to the chase.

Jadwiga was a very well-remunerated performer, with her own trailer and staff at the circus. She only worked three months of the year; that's how well-remunerated. Her marriage of three years to a fellow dwarf called Heathcliff (another stage name) had gone from bad to worse after the honeymoon.

Heathcliff was a dwarf clown who specialised in aerial and wire work and drove the exploding car that was the clowns' act climax. At 4'4" he was fully six inches taller than Jadwiga and he threw his weight around mercilessly until she got help to throw him out of her trailer. Now he lived in another trailer, less well-appointed, close to the potbellied Siamese pigs, other stars of the show. He was a brutal cruel psycho. But I'm getting ahead of myself.

I had two tasks here at Frankie & Benny's. First, to get my feelings under control so that my intensifying infatuation with Jadwiga would not cloud my professional judgement. And second, to design and execute a scheme to kill an irascible dwarf in a way that would not have witnesses able to trace the plot back to me and Jadwiga. We also had to agree a fee, though this was soon ranking a very low third in my priorities. The whole business began to take on an obsessive character.

———

Call me Zack. I should probably tell you a bit more about myself. I get all my work as a cleaner through the dark web. My clients are always shocked the first time they see me even though the disclaimers and explanations are all there on my website with my credentials. Somehow none of it ever seems to make a difference. I see their faces get away from them every time . The eyes widen a bit in surprise. A quickly suppressed smile sometimes. Or the jaw suddenly sets in a kind of taut shock. Anyway.

My IQ is in the region of 200 which is the score they put on me before I saw the downside of the whole profiling thing and learned to fake the test to come in lower. I'm not quite 11 years old at the time of writing this. I can't wait to hit puberty, I've heard great things about it.

I live at home with my Mum. The guy who calls himself my father is away much of the week in London, working for a blue-chip global firm everyone has heard of. Whatever.

This suits me just fine ever since I engineered the temporary exclusion order from that crap school with all those dumb dorks and the even dumber headmistress. Mum is either stuck to her screen during the day or out at one of her business breakfasts or Pilates or networking gigs for her interior design business. This so-called lifestyle is the perfect cover for me and my business.

———

This dwarf Heathcliff was not going to be a pushover to kill, I could see that immediately.

For a start he was hideously strong. Part of his act

involved throwing around 25kg kettle bells as if they were featherweights. It always got a gasp from the crowd. He would pick up one of these in a pincer grip and hoist it over his head one-handed. You would think it was a paper mache fake. But actually it was the real deal

Being a kid is often a fantastic asset in my work. So it proved this time.

No one does a double-take at a kid in short trousers mooching around at the circus, in the Big Top or even out by the generator trucks. I took the precaution of wearing a school cap and munching (probably quite redundantly) on a huge ball of candy floss to hide much of my face most of the time. In this fashion I was able to carry out pretty much the perfect recce during a matinee show at Dart's Circus.

I noticed that there would be an interval after Heathcliff staggered spluttering from the exploding car in the centre of the ring, once the wheels and doors flew off, and before he reached the curtains at the back of the tent. I would have a clear line of sight to him if I could only get the end aisle seat. The plumes of white smoke drifting from his clown car might also be helpful for what I had in mind. There would be other people around me, no doubt, because Dart's Circus was always a complete sell-out and tickets were gold dust. But I was confident I'd find a way around that when it came to the moment.

———

I used a customised razor and secateurs to cut a single schoolboy-sized slit just big enough to let me in and out of the Big Top. I returned after dark to do this and it went well enough although the dogs barking around the nearby trailer were bothering me at first. But nobody investigated.

The job took a bit longer than I'd figured. It was raining and the cold damp air on my numb hands slowed me down with the razor and the secateurs. I used clear-plastic sticking plasters to hold the newly cut seams in place. You would have to be looking specially for the cut to see it when I'd finished.

Worst of it all was that Mum was waiting when I got back to the house and she did one about my being missing for a couple of hours (she got back unexpectedly early from one of her bookclub evenings with her pals).

I had to make up some bullshit story on the spot about checking out the rainfall conservation science project in the woods not that far away from our house. She stopped shouting and crying "Zack Zack" eventually, choosing to accept my bullshit tale and maybe part-persuaded by the fact that I was still soaking wet in my school gabardine. Thank God she didn't check my backpack with the cutting gear still in it. And the Anglo Arms Gecko Crossbow, a lightweight modern weapon which develops 87 foot pounds of energy for a bolt travelling at 300 feet per second.

I always keep a log of jobs and I never needed it more than I do now. I don't think they - the cops - can trace me. But that's the only good thing about this one. I have to get it all down here, a kind of "Dear Diary" otherwise I'll go insane, I know I will. Oh my God, why did I ever take this one on? Oh my poor poor Jadwiga. I'm so sorry my love.

———

It all went swimmingly at first. The end seats were occupied by a pack of about six infants and their two teenage girl carers. The girls were giggly and chatting all the time and checking their phones in an orgy of distraction. Two people less likely to notice things or to act as reliable witnesses it would be hard to find. I even had time to remove the clear band-aids to make the unobtrusive get-away easier, it would be a simple matter to slip out of the tent in the confusion.

Heathcliff was at his demonic best during his act hurling those weights around. Then the wheels and doors flew off the car at the climax. He bellowed and flopped out of the exploding vehicle onto the sawdust, energetically flapping his elongated clown sneaker-flippers. He headed for the back of the tent waving his arms as if distracted and blind in the smoke.

Under cover of the mock-satchel on my lap, specially adapted for the purpose, I steadied the hidden crossbow with its bolt for the single shot. The sight-line was ideal, I had practised it to perfection.

There was a blur of motion speeding past Heathcliff, something that had not happened at the rehearsal matinee. Too late for me to abort the shot. Heathcliff turned his head suddenly to see Jadwiga on a unicycle rushing past him to the centre of the circus ring. The bolt hissed by him so close it nicked his Adam's apple. His eyes were bulging alarmingly. The bolt shot past him and buried itself up to the tail feathers in Jadwiga's side just under her left breast, piercing her heart.

The tent went quiet. Then the screaming began.

MIGUEL

JACK D MCLEAN

He stood by his car looking my way. Faceless at this distance with the heat turning the highway into a gleaming river, the scorching desert air blurring him and his vehicle into a single shimmering object.

The two of us were the only people around for fifty miles or more.

Whenever I'm alone with someone I ask myself whether that might present an opportunity. As I approached him I realised it probably did.

His car, a blue Trans-Am, was parked in the dirt to one side of the highway.

I guessed he'd broken down. As I got closer I saw he looked Mexican, like me, which wasn't surprising as I was on that side of the border, having recently left the good ol' USA in something of a hurry.

Due to a robbery gone wrong I was on the run. Didn't have any plans but at least I'd gotten away with enough cash to pay for whatever I needed for the next few months.

He waved his arms in the air in the universally-recognised signal that you want attention. He'd got it. I put my foot on the brake to slow down and he lowered his arms, stepping sideways out of my path.

At the last moment I pressed my foot fully on the gas, turned the wheel, and accelerated directly at him.

He tried to run but his own vehicle got in the way. I caught him a forceful blow and he fell in the dirt. With clouds of dust flying up from the rapidly revolving wheels of my car, I put it into reverse and crushed his midriff. It was doubtful he was still alive after that but I ran over him another couple of times to make sure. One of those times I went clean over his face with a front wheel.

I stopped and checked out his car. The key was in the ignition. When I turned it the light came on telling me the gas tank was empty. Chances were there was nothing wrong with the car. Just needed filling up.

I opened the cajuela, removed my case of car thieving gear, and took out the device I use for syphoning off petrol. Then I siphoned about a litre out of my car and put it into his. When I tried the ignition again the engine fired to life.

Having convinced myself I could make use of his car I put the rest of my gas in his tank and emptied his pockets. He had a wallet with his driver's licence in it. His name was Miguel Hernandez and he wasn't Mexican. He was American like me, and a Latino like me. I swapped his wallet for mine, my keys for his. Then I emptied my car and put the contents in his, and vice-versa, and drove away, leaving his corpse next to my car.

Chances were he'd be found, his face crushed to a

pulp, and the Mexican police would look at his id and assume he was me. The Texan cops wouldn't question it. They'd just be grateful another perp had been killed and another case could be closed.

So I got into my new Trans-Am feeling pretty good about things. Then it occurred to me he might have more worth stealing. I looked in his wallet, found where he lived, and decided to check the place out.

It meant heading North, back the way I'd come on Highway 150D, towards Mexico City. I punched "Go Home" into his GPS and followed the virtual car on the screen, eventually turning into the quiet street in the upmarket suburb where he lived. By the time I arrived it was dark, and the clear night sky was an inky blue dotted with stars.

It was a nice wide road with big detached houses set well back, all of them white with red tiled roofs, big windows, and imposing front doors. I drove straight to his, turning into the drive, and confidently parking on it. Driving his car with my looks, at night, chances were that anyone looking out his window would've taken me for him.

It was obvious he had money and hopefully some of it was in his house, or something else worth stealing.

Was anyone in?

There were no lights on at the front of the house. I felt for the reassuring bulge of my gun in my shoulder holster and when I'd pointlessly convinced myself it was still there, I got out of the car as if I owned the place and went right up to the door. Then I pulled out the keys I'd taken from him and tried a couple in the lock. The second worked and I pushed the door open as quietly as I could then pulled it gently shut behind me.

I switched on the lights. I figured it's what Miguel would've done and I wanted his neighbours to assume I was him.

First thing I did was draw the curtains keeping my head down so that if anyone looked through the window at me, all they'd see was my hair which was black, like his. After that I searched the front room. Nothing of interest. But it was a big house with a few downstairs rooms. I checked them all. They were expensively furnished but nothing jumped out at me as small and valuable enough to be worth putting in my car.

So I went upstairs. Figured that's where the money was likely to be hidden if there was any. Sure enough there was a safe which I couldn't open. And a bank of computers in a bedroom – like you'd expect of someone who played the stock market. Or a money launderer.

A drawer in a dressing table yielded a couple of piles of fifty dollar bills secured by rubber bands. They found a new home in the side pockets of my jacket. It was time to leave, quit while I was ahead. So I made my way out casually as if I was in no big hurry, got in the car and glided to the end of the street.

Once I'd turned the corner I put my foot on the gas and screeched the hell out of there.

Soon Mexico City was behind me and I was heading south towards Acapulco on Highway 95D. It seemed as good a destination as any in my current circumstances.

The hotel I booked into was good but not over-the-top as I didn't want to attract a lot of attention to myself, especially as I paid for my room with Miguel's credit card. I took my few things up there, had a shower, then strolled out to buy some urgently needed items—clothes, a suitcase, and so on, as, leaving town the way I had done, there hadn't been time to pack. When I returned to my room the door slammed shut behind me, without me doing the shutting.

I turned, at the same time reaching for my gun. Saw two men who'd been at the back of the door. One of them swung at my head with a blackjack. I tried to step back, create space to defend myself, but he was too quick for me, and it was lights out baby.

I wasn't unconscious though I might as well have been because I had a splitting headache and couldn't do anything other than lie on the floor groaning.

When I got to my feet it wasn't under my own steam. The welcoming committee had relieved me of my gun and hauled me upright. They took me down a back staircase to a parked car, shoved me in it, and set off to an unknown destination.

It turned out to be a wooden shack in the desert.

They dragged me from the car, got me inside, and tied me to a wooden chair.

By that time I was just about able to talk.

"What-what's this all about?"

One of them, a sadistic-looking Mexican bastard with bad teeth, a skinny face, and greasy hair, said:

"You know what it's about, amigo. Juan Carlos sent us. He's not a happy man, as you know."

"Juan Carlos?"

"Your employer. The man you are meant to be laundering money for. You remember him?"

"What? No. There's been a mistake."

"There is no mistake amigo, except for the one you made. It was a very big mistake to take money from Juan Carlos and think you could get away with it. Now he has to make an example of you to make sure no-one else makes such a mistake."

"Wait, wait. I'm not the man you think I am!"

He laughed.

"Have you heard this Rafael? He's not who we think he is."

Both men laughed.

"You won't escape your fate, Miguel, no matter how clever your excuses are."

"But I'm not Miguel."

"Oh, Rafael, he's clever, eh? But he's forgotten he was carrying his id in his jacket."

"I'm really not Miguel."

He shook his head.

"It doesn't matter who you are. Your fate is sealed. It is sealed whether or not you tell us what you did with the money. But you can make things better for yourself by telling us everything. Your death can be slow and very painful, or quick. If you tell us what we want to know it will be quick. If you don't..." he shook his head. Then he pulled back his fist and punched me in the face. Hard.

It took me by surprise. My head snapped back and a slew of blood flew from my mouth.

"That is what pain feels like, Miguel," he said. "And it is only the beginning."

His cell phone bleeped. He put it to his ear.

"Yes? Yes? All right. We are on our way."

He returned the cell to his pocket.

"We have to go now, Miguel. We'll be back. Don't go anywhere."

They both laughed and went out the door.
I don't know when they'll be back.
Fucking Miguel.
Why did he do this to me?

The End

GETTING OVER JEN

JACK D MCLEAN

Jake_C_T Ryan@googlemail.com
08/03/2017
To: Deborah..Shine@hotmail.co.uk

Hi Deborah,

How are you?

I saw your Facebook profile and was very impressed. My name is Jake Ryan and I'm a marine with the US armed forces. I've served in various parts of the world and I do peacekeeping work in Kabul, in Afghanistan.

Right now I'm on leave in England, in your hometown – Huddersfield and I was wondering if we could hook up?
We have a lot in common and your profile says you'd like to meet a military man.

If you want to know about me, I'm a stand-up guy who'd never let you down.

I've been in the marines for nearly 27 years, and I'm coming up for retirement very soon.

When I retire I'll be starting a new life as a civilian and it would be great if I could start it with a woman like you.
You say you like curry. My favourite foods are curries and I've become partial to your English craft beers.

I've attached a couple of photos of myself. I hope you like what you see.

Would you like to tell me a bit about yourself?

Thank you so much, I look forward to receiving your response.

My warmest regards
Jake

———

Deborah..Shine@hotmail.co.uk
08/03/2017
To:
Jake_C_T Ryan@googlemail.com

Dear Jake,

Thank you for your delightful email. I can't tell you

how thrilled I was to receive it. To be honest with you, I've been going through a hard time lately because a close friend of mine died, and your message really gave me a boost.
Of course I'd love to meet you.

Here's an interesting fact about me: I'm partial to craft beers myself, especially pale ale. Here's another: I'm free to meet during the day, which would be perfect as you're on leave.

Since you like curries, how about I cook you one? I could come to your place with the ingredients and you could get some craft ales to drink with it.

Tomorrow would be good for me. I could drop in on you about, say, 12:00 noon and spend an hour cooking for you. Then we could eat, have a chat, and get to know each other.
How about it?

And if you're up for it, what's your address?

Best wishes,
Deborah

———

Jake_C_T Ryan@googlemail.com
08/03/2017
To: Deborah..Shine@hotmail.co.uk

Hi Deborah,

Thank you for getting back to me so quickly.

That would be great!

I'm staying in apartment 5 at Meridian House in St George's Square.

See you tomorrow at noon!

I'll have some beers chilling in the fridge!!!

Warmest regards and thank you so much – you've made my day!

Jake

———

Jake_C_T Ryan@googlemail.com
14/03/2017
To: Deborah..Shine@hotmail.co.uk

Hi Deborah,

Unfortunately I can't meet with you today. I seem to be coming down with the 'flu. I'll get in touch as soon as I'm feeling better.

Love
Jake

———

Deborah..Shine@hotmail.co.uk
14/03/2017
To:
Jake_C_T Ryan@googlemail.com

Dear Jake,

Sorry to hear about your bout of 'flu.

And thank you for a wonderful afternoon! I really enjoyed meeting you.

I promised I'd get some money for you, but I'm not going to bother. There'd be no point. I'll explain why.

I'll also explain why I wouldn't have sex with you. I told you I was on my period but frankly, that was a lie.

Deborah Shine isn't my real name. This isn't my real email provider. And the IP address I'm using isn't in any detectable way connected to me.

My close friend Jen (not her real name) was ripped off by a man like you. She committed suicide.

Ever since, it's been my personal mission to make the world a safer place for women by removing your sort from the surface of the planet.

You don't have the 'flu.

You've eaten a hearty portion of Lamb Thallium.

Sorry about the messy death that's coming your way soon.

Yours truly,
Deborah

The End

THE GIANT RAT OF SUMATRA AND ZACK

MARTIN MULLIGAN

The Giant Rat of Sumatra: that was his handle in the trade. A name uttered in an awed whisper. A mythic figure who left living leg-ends, still twitching and pulsing blood, at his kill-sites. (He liked to work with an axe.) Half-Indonesian, half-Russian, they said he stood six and a half feet tall and came in at a fighting weight of nearly 300 pounds. He once straightened a bent poker with his bare hands in front of guests by the roaring fireplace of a five-star Alpine lodge (their Russian oligarch host was found headless in bed the next morning).

The Giant Rat of Sumatra, in brief, was not the sort of guy you want to cross - let alone to have to try to "eliminate". But it was pretty clear by now that it was going to be him or me. And I'm only a schoolboy, for God's sake, I should be out collecting Pokemon!

Let's go back a bit to put this thing in perspective. Who, you ask, would want to kill a ginger-top, freckled, bespectacled, not-quite 12-year-old schoolkid who just happens to have a part-time freelance identity working from home?

Plenty of people, actually, if that kid happens to be a prepubescent propeller-head (with an IQ above 200) specialised in confidential murder that carries a hefty price-tag. Also with an international network and an offshore account in the Caymans. I know, I know. Cue all those polymath-prodigy, boy-wonder detective jokes about the precocious schoolboy in an exurban setting. It's even funnier when you learn that, though he lives at home with his Mum, he was on the rebound from having his heart broken by a circus dwarf. (But that's another story.)

It all started with an email I made the mistake of opening instead of sending straight to Trash. But I get most of my work this way, so sometimes I have no choice but to override my instincts. Anyway. The sender wanted to know if I could find a source of Red Mercury. The promised fee was colossal. It had to be. Red Mercury is underworld slang for fuel from decommissioned nuclear power stations. It has no peaceful - nor even any harmless - applications. I ought to have binned the email a second time when I saw that phrase. But I didn't.

So I was suddenly neck-deep in a classical crime-story dilemma. As the prospective victim, that did nothing to console me. I had followed up a job lead that I should have deleted instantly. Now I knew too much and was in too deep to extricate myself without serious consequences. Fatal consequences, in fact. Fatal, that is, to me.

The bullet-points, then: I was still broken-hearted after Jadwiga; so crazy-busy with my criminal career that it had affected my judgment; and now in way over my head with a Chechnyan terrorist organisation that no-one else even knew existed. I didn't like to think about what they meant to do with the Red Mercury if they actually got hold of any. But the question was academic. My energy was focussed on getting myself out of this atomic mess alive and in one piece. No simple matter when you happen to be going up against the most feared ambush predator in the business. Of course, waiting in the wings, there was also my complex home and school life. But we'll get to that.

———

The news that the Giant Rat of Sumatra was coming to kill me leaked out by accident. It was only a freakish chance that I heard about it at all, before I ended up like his countless other victims, just another mayfly spattered on the windshield of a speeding truck.

It happened like this. An alcoholic informer-turned-supergrass (Stoyan Stoyanovich was his alias, I had used him one time on a job in Sofia) called me from a wine-cellar somewhere in the Balkans. We spoke only for about 90 seconds but my hand was shaking when I put my moby back in my pocket. So that was it, then. They had given the Giant Rat of Sumatra my "contact details". They had even wired the money for the assignment to him in advance.

To give you some idea why my hands were shaking, here's one of the stories in circulation about the Giant Rat. It's the sort of thing people in my line of work gossip about sometimes over a late-night drink in a hotel lobby in Manila or a Chicago bar.

While he was still a rookie crook, the young and beardless Giant Rat of Sumatra was given a support role in a hit on a capo in a Little Italy restaurant in Manhattan. He was to act as lookout and getaway driver. But a tip-off meant that the capo and his people were expecting the hit squad when they burst into the busy restaurant at lunch hour. Each member of the hit squad died horribly on the spot. Meanwhile three of the capo's crew, all toting handguns, ambushed the juvenile Giant Rat further up the block as he sat waiting behind the wheel of the getaway car. They made the mistake of thinking that because he was only a kid (granted, a very big kid) they could take him in for questioning. He stepped from the car with his hands raised, shucked out the tyre-iron hidden in his sleeve and beat out the brains of all three assailants. He left them on the kerb looking like the Three Piggies. (Three body-doubles, that is, of Piggy from Lord of the Flies.) You get the idea. The rest of his career had amply fulfilled the early promise this episode showed. You see now why I was nervous.

Reckoning up the pros and cons, it seemed to me that one of my very few advantages was that the Giant Rat of Sumatra was bound to be conspicuous in my sleepy leafy green exurban village. It would not be easy for him to get close to me without attracting attention. So he would have to be quick about it and almost certainly in disguise. It was laughable, in a way. How do you disguise yourself if you happen to be a hulking, tank-like man, with the dimensions of a Sumo wrestler, trying to blend in plausibly in a prosperous suburban milieu in the South of England? A place teeming with artisan coffee shops and eco-friendly delis, village greensward, cobbled squares, art galleries, and honey-coloured ancient churches. It was going to be fascinating to find out (even though he was coming expressly to kill me).

———

It helped that I was off school for a few days with one of my "mystery ailments". In order to devote myself to the secret life of a "cleaner" operating via the dark web, I have to skive off school quite frequently. This was one of those times. It also played right into my hands that my Mum was away for two nights at a Grand Designs conference in London, leaving me momentarily a latchkey kid. That all suited me just fine. But by Friday, I had to be back in the classroom or there would be ructions from the school authorities. I could not allow that to happen. I can't have people looking too closely into my lifestyle. Also, my Mum was not around to make me sandwiches. So by Friday, when the Giant Rat had still not made his move, a combination of ennui and hunger drove me back to the school's precincts.

The bell sounded for school-dinner time. Never an occasion I enjoyed but I had been living for most of a week on Shreddies and salad-cream sandwiches. I headed for the dining hall. Collapsible tables, tureens and resonating surfaces, all very well-lit. Not a setting I looked forward to occupying, since I'd endured far too many lacklustre meals and schoolboy skirmishes in that place over the years. But I shrugged my shoulders in my coarse black blazer and got in line for cottage pie at the first serving hatch.

The kid in front of me was a sleazy sixth former who really fancied himself. He was having some sort of exchange, loaded with innuendo, with a louche giggling dinner lady who wore too much makeup. "I do like a tart now and then," he was smirking at her, "a custard tart, of course". I could see clearly the woman he was talking to off to my right. Their silly exchange distracted me for a moment so that I wasn't looking straight ahead at the other dinner lady directly facing me at the hatch. When I turned my head, intending to ask for the cottage pie (not the pasta), I saw no face but only a dangling lanyard at normal head-height. It bore an ID snap and the words: Matilda Briggs Supply Dinner Staff.

In that awful moment before I was sure, as I read the plastic lanyard dangling from the huge figure's neck and craned my neck to see its face, I skipped reflexively backwards. It was a lifesaving move. A sharpened spade-like serving-spoon cleaved the air like a scythe where my head had been only a nanosecond ago.

I was staring at the biggest bulkiest dinner lady you ever saw, in a starched white apron with the circumference of an igloo. Blonde hair in ringlets spilled on to the figure's improbably broad shoulders. The eyes were nearly hidden under a fringe of the same stuff.

Yes, the rabid-looking, bewigged Giant Rat of Sumatra was preparing to lunge through the serving hatch to crush me in a grizzly hug.

I had to take the battle to him somehow. I threw myself at the serving hatch and saw a flicker of surprise cross my hulking assailant's face. He had expected me to run. Instead, I vaulted nimbly through the hatch, grazing his hippo-like thigh as I sailed past to land about a metre behind his back, before he had time to pivot.

Fumbling with my wristwatch, I managed to deploy the tungsten steel-wire garrotte attached to the winding button watch-fob. All that playground ridicule from my peers about my Mickey Mouse watch was suddenly worthwhile. It had cost a fortune to commission from an illegal specialist but I had always felt in my bones that it would repay me big-time one of these days.

With another leap I managed to flip the watch-garrotte over his pumpkin of a head and loop it around his columnar neck. Then it was all I could do to stay in place on his back as the wire bit deep and he started to buck and thrash like a huge marlin at sea.

Oh, he was a jolly brawler. He dived through the serving hatch with me on his back. We must have looked like something straight out of a Disney version of Jonah and the Whale. The garrotte was tightening and already starting to hurt my my wrists and arms. He landed on all fours with a behemoth's bellow of pain and rage, reared up and drove like a snowplough through the dining room tables, scattering plates of pasta and cottage pie in all directions, to screams and shouts now. I was somehow still clinging to his back like an infant rodeo-rider. But we couldn't go on like this, it was ridiculous.

I caught sight of the head teacher entering the hall with a mouth like an "O" and both hands up to her face. The Giant Rat of Sumatra barrelled past her, with me pretty much concealed like a limpet on his broad heaving back. He struck a pillar in Reception with his shoulder and gave vent to another roar of pain. Which I echoed shrilly, since the pillar caught me a raking blow on the left side of my head as we went by.

The impact shook me loose, my hands numb from clutching the Mickey Mouse watch-garrotte that had left a wound pouring a thin curtain of blood from the Giant Rat's neck and throat. He smashed the school entrance doors open and stormed up the drive like a bull-elephant wearing a starched white apron. Then he vanished out of the front gate (outside which a huge blonde wig was found by police later that day).

There were questions, of course, endless questions. In the confusion, all that anyone had seen was me seeming to leap into the kitchen through the service hatch. Then a huge madman rampaged through the dining hall. Other kids had been knocked aside and panicked by the Giant Rat's stampede. Some of them were hysterical and voluble, mercifully taking the spotlight off me. (That blubbering wuss Adrian Gapper-Johnson, for instance, was a godsend. He was covered in bruises, gravy and mince and shrieking for his mother as the policewoman tried to calm him.)

I told the head mistress and police that I had just clung to the "nasty man's" sleeve, milking for all it was worth that childish fantasy of the Famous Five have-a-go hero (all I was missing was Timmy the dog in support). Nobody thought to connect me to the episode in any deeper way because it made no sense unless you knew about my secret life. Everyone was instead deeply concerned about me. I was able to make a mountain out of the molehill-bump on my left temple. The skin had torn and it looked quite impressive. All the same, I was relieved when they finally sent me home in the police car and let me skip the afternoon's classes (ukulele and computing).

A very inept police artist's impression of the Giant Rat was pinned to the notice board in Reception on Monday morning when we all pitched up for assembly. That I had put a scratch on him only made matters worse, I thought to myself. In my line of work, it's never a good idea to hurt what you can't kill. He would be angrier now. Perhaps that would cloud his judgment and be in my favour. But I needed backup, that much was certain. So it was a good moment to call Bob the Jinx.

Bob the Jinx runs a plumber's-merchant depot in a neighbouring town about four miles away. I cycled over on my All Terrain bike as soon as school was over. I have a carbon -frame model that is sturdy but lightweight and it's my chief way of exercising and transport, so I'm pretty agile on it.

The shop bell rang with an old-fashioned tinkling chime when I pressed the brass button by the heavy oak door. After a long moment, while the hidden camera scanned me, Bob the Jinx let me in. You can't be too careful these days in his metier, for which the plumbers'-merchant screen is the perfect camouflage. Bob the Jinx is the go-to guy when you have a problem like the one I had. Kevlar body armour, automatic weaponry, surveillance gear, Claymore mines; you name it, Bob the Jinx would get it (if he didn't already have it). And he would sell it to you for an eye-watering price tag. In short, I understood and liked the guy. (Bob the Jinx it was who had provided me with my Mickey Mouse garrotte-watch.)

Bob the Jinx was busy welding something in a vice at the back of his dusty, gloomy shop. He pushed up his visor and took off his reversed baseball cap to wipe his brow when I approached.

"Hey, Bob", I said.

"Zack. Long time. How is everything?"

I told him in a few broad brush-strokes about the Giant Rat of Sumatra and my "situation". He whistled softly at the mention of the celebrated assassin. I told Bob the Jinx that I would be needing a few items, one or two of them customised. He is very dependable in a fix. He listened intently, jotted a few notes on a tablet and told me to come back in a couple of hours. By seven o'clock, I was back home with the necessaries that Bob the Jinx had provided in an awkward, angular, very heavy ruck sack.

My plan required that the next time the Giant Rat tried to kill me should be after dark. To that end, I started cycling around at night on my Avenir Voodoo AT20 Series, ensuring that my lights and ruby red reflectors were seen all over the village. They became a commonplace sight. Other kids were out, too, some of them also on bikes, which was all to the good. I was still visible but I didn't look like a human lure. Yet an irresistible bait for the Great Rat of Sumatra is precisely what I was aiming to be.

East of the village, right by the deep, fast-flowing Iris River, is an industrial estate which houses storage units and a few local business offices: a print shop; a warehouse; office space to let, that sort of thing. A typical exurban science park. A post-industrial soulless wasteland, one of those in-between places nobody visits at night or at the weekend. I got down there soon after dark and set to work on a grass slope hidden by hawthorn bushes that led steeply (at a nearly vertiginous drop) to the river.

It all took quite a bit of setting up. It was vital that nothing should be visible from the street corner a hundred yards away, no matter how sharply a driver took the corner. I was working by flashlight, and that was making the job much harder than it would have been in daylight. A couple of hours or so went by before I was completely confident the device and its accessories that Bob the Jinx had made and primed for me were properly set up and installed. I went back home, then, to finish my homework and to have a Mexican meal with my Mum. She was back now from her London conference and talked endlessly about it over supper before she crashed out early.

For four evenings like this I cycled around Wychwode as soon as the street lights came on and dusk descended. Nothing. I was beginning to wonder if I'd miscalculated. Then, on Friday night, something happened.

I was too far away from the site I'd marked out for my countermeasures, really, and it nearly cost me my life. Maybe I was beginning to doubt my own plan or just losing heart after the long wait. Cycling around muddy reclaimed land to the west of Wychwode, I was getting ready to call it a day and to abandon my role as a lure. Then I heard it: a siren, some way off. An ambulance siren. Uh-oh. I knew enough about his

MO and his criminal driver's pedigree to join the dots at once.

I began to pedal like crazy in the opposite direction, away from the ambulance noise. I was making directly for the science park in the east village. The siren was louder now. It was also full night already and a thin drizzle had begun to fall as I took the long curving road to the industrial estate and hammered past the mini roundabout. The siren was, I reckoned, only about a minute behind me now. I turned to risk a swift look.

Sure enough, a green-white ambulance with flashing lights was blaring its shrill note about 30 seconds behind me. Too distant still to be sure who was at the wheel but I didn't need to be told. This had the Giant Rat of Sumatra's signature all over it. If it turned out not to be him, I would just have to take on myself the bad karma of what happened next; the situation left me no choice. But in my heart I knew it was him. I knew it with the absolute certainty of someone trapped like a trap in a trap.

The steady drizzle was impairing visibility, blurring everything behind a hazy curtain in the sodium glare of the street lights which thinned out closer to the industrial estate.

Everything would hinge on my timing. The Giant Rat could only have an indistinct view of me and my bike from behind as I hung a sharp left and plunged off the road toward the hawthorn hedge and the slope.

I leaned into a sliding skid that flung the bike off away under me, letting it go wherever it would, timing my own spread-eagle sliding body-skid to bury myself deep out of sight of the road among the trunks of the hawthorn trees. I was about 20 yards away from where I had set up the trap. If the ambulance driver slammed on his anchors now it would mean the Giant Rat had somehow picked me out clearly despite the rain and the dark. Then the game would be up and I'd be finished.

The ambulance shot past, siren still going. He'd missed me! He had taken the bait! Just as I'd planned, the ambulance dopplered maniacally past me in my hiding place straight toward the winking ruby-red reflector on the camouflaged tripod that Bob the Jinx had custom-engineered to my specifications, set up so painstakingly in the hawthorn bushes by the river-slope. Driving at speed in the rainy dark, the Giant Rat thought he still saw my tail-light. He had swerved suddenly off-road (swearing horribly no doubt) to crush and annihilate bike and rider.

I heard the dull thump of the Claymore going off as the ambulance shot through the screen of bushes (carrying with it on a fender the reflector that resembled my tail light).

The vaulting mine's shrapnel took out the windscreen and most of the driver's offside, strafing the driver's cabin with a deadly hail and a force that tilted the ambulance sideways in mid-air.

The great white vehicle described a lazy arc in the night, headlights strobing for a second the river beneath. Those dark deep deadly waters. Those fearsome fatal rat-drowning waters. The siren warbled to a sudden silence as the river's strong, lazy current took the sinking ambulance in its near-zero chill embrace.

The bats flittered, the field mice chittered by the hither and thithering waters of the River Iris, its waters cold, colder, coldest as the Giant Rat went down to his rest. The headlights dimmed, then died, and all was still except for a final muted dull heavy gurgling as the vehicle sank out of sight underwater, its descent marked fleetingly by a metallic oily bubbling vortex.

The Giant Rat of Sumatra didn't die that night. But only in the sense that a legend never dies. The corpse of an infamous Indonesian-Russian murderer was recovered from the wreck of a stolen ambulance when it came to light weeks later. These days the stories retold after dark by my peers in bars from Singapore to Chicago are about me.

The End

JUSTICE

JACK D MCLEAN

My trial comes up next week and I could be facing a life sentence. My son's dead worried about it but I'm not. I can't wait to see that bastard Sykes in court testifying against me, telling the world what I did to him. I can't wait to see the look on his face when it's over and he realises what I've done.

I'm a retired businessman. I shouldn't have got drawn into committing a crime at my age but when my grandson died, I had no choice. He was only four years old.

The wife was in bits and as for my son, Alan, and my daughter-in-law, Beth, they'll never get over it.

Have you ever seen a child's coffin? They're so tiny. It breaks your heart, it really does.

It was how little Eddie died that got to me as much as anything.

He was riding his tricycle when a truck came up the road and took the corner too tight. The rear wheel mounted the pavement and ran over my little Eddie.

He banged his head when he fell and never recovered.

People who saw the accident said the driver – Harry Sykes laughed when he realised what he'd done.

He got prosecuted for it, and said he was sorry but it was just an act. He might've pulled the wool over the Judge's eyes, but not mine. I knew he was saying it just to get off – and it worked.

The prosecution charged Sykes with causing death by careless driving. It should've been murder if you ask me.

It was his first offence so he got a suspended sentence and walked out of court a free man.

What kind of justice is that?

He ought to have been banged up for years.

So I decided to do something about it.

I had a word with the wife. We agreed I should take the law into my own hands.

But I didn't discuss it with my son. He wouldn't have understood. Alan is a very different person to me. I've had to claw my way up from the gutter to get on in life and he's had all the privileges you can get from day one.

When he was growing up I put an expensive roof over his head, made sure he had good food to eat, and paid for him to have the best education going. He went to university and became a successful lawyer. He doesn't know anything about the sacrifices I've had to make on his behalf. I gave up everything for my family, including a few scruples along the way.

Once I'd decided to avenge Eddie's death I went out and brought a gun. A 38 snub nose revolver, a real Saturday night special.

When I confronted Sykes in the street he tried to use his girlfriend as a shield.

"Be a man," I said walking up close and holding the gun against his temple.

But he cowered like a frightened little girl, got to his knees, and begged for mercy.

"Please, I don't know why you're doing this, let me live."

"It's for my grandson, Eddie. The little boy you killed. Remember him?"

I crouched down, put the muzzle to his thigh, and pulled the trigger.

There was a deafening noise as the gun went off.

The bullet shattered his thighbone. When I pulled the gun away there was a big hole in the side of his leg with wisps of smoke coming out of it.

Very nasty.

His girlfriend screamed and he screamed even louder.

"Serves you right you cunt," I told him.

I turned to his girlfriend.

"Sorry about that, love," I said. "I didn't mean to drag you into this but I had no choice. If he was half a man he wouldn't have used you as a shield and you wouldn't have had to see this. You ought to finish with him. You've seen what he's like. He's no good."

I put the gun in my waistband and walked away.

It wasn't long before the coppers came round to my gaff and arrested me.

They charged me with causing Grievous Bodily Harm. The sentence for that is almost as bad as that for murder. So in some ways I might as well have killed Sykes. But I wanted him to live, to feel the pain I felt.

I didn't deny the charge. How could I? I did it in broad daylight on the high street. Lots of people saw me and it was recorded on video.

It's been hard on my son, of course.

"Dad, how could you?" He said. "Why did you take the law into your own hands? You should know better than that. You used to be a respected businessman. I've lost Eddie, and now I'm going to lose you. You'll be locked up for this."

"Sorry, son," I said. "Don't worry. I'll get a good brief. He'll get me off."

"You don't know what you're talking about. It's an open and shut case. You'll get sent down for years."

"Suppose you're right."

But I knew he wasn't.

You see, my line of business was extortion and racketeering, using extreme violence as a means of persuasion.

And by the time my mates get through with the jury, they'll be awarding me a medal, never mind letting me off.

The End

MOVING ON

MARTIN MULLIGAN

Most Tuesday nights I like to watch our wedding video again. The fashions have changed out of all recognition in 30 years. Those bouffant hairstyles of the men and women alike in the 1980s! Nearly everyone in the video is dead now, of course. Or they are friends we long since lost touch with. Even the cars parked outside the church look strange from this distance in time. (One of my uncles, Ben, showed up open-necked and had to blag a tie from me. Then he drove at about 20 mph in a Ford Fiesta all the way to the reception venue, causing a half-mile tailback on the busy A-road.) As bride and groom we left, chauffeur-driven, in a white vintage Hispano Suiza that had once belonged to the Archduke Franz Ferdinand.

I don't know how I first got the idea that it would be good to burn things to the ground. To start afresh from the ashes of the world. Pyromaniac. What a beautiful word.

I like the girl in the artisan coffee shop here in Wychwode. She has long blonde hair in ringlets and a strange accent. Her name badge has "Matilda" on it. Last week she even gave me a free second cup. It turned out to be a mistake and so I paid for it anyway in the end. But still. The other staff behind the counter are all cyphers. But I really liked that she brought me a second coffee at all as I sat there watching the passers-by on the sunlit street outside from my regular window seat.

I was reading about paints and solvents and taking notes. It's easy to blend in there with all the bespectacled guys working on their laptops and ordering yet another tall skinny latte and croissant.

On the way back to my house from the coffee shop, I dropped into Red Kite Vaults, the village vintners run by Derek and his assistant Jack. Their relationship always tickles me. Derek is the Antipodean proprietor and sole owner of Red Kite Vaults. He always refers to Jack (behind Jack's back, of course) as "Jack who *works* here". But I like Jack, a small docile family man with large moppet-like brown eyes. Jack loves to get out and about on the occasional wine-buying trip to France or Italy. I think I'm going to find it quite hard when the time comes to put petrol through their letter box.

You would never expect it, never expect this, to be suddenly catapulted into the life of a Balzac novel, like an elderly miser on his death-bed surrounded by the vultures of his relatives and so-called friends and colleagues, even virtual strangers, all circling, you can almost hear their claws clicking, their beaks snapping. All because of the Monkey's Paw effect when your partner dies, the policies vest, everything changes. Worth more dead than alive: that old cliche. But not actually a cliche, it is rather a truth tired with iteration, it's cropping up the whole time in our society, the way we live now. Nor is it helpful to deny it, to pretend that things, that people, are in fact better than they are. Better just to accept, don't fight it, let it rise in consciousness in all its painful ugliness, just stay with it, watching. *"The Way of the Warrior entails walking the razor's edge,"* as they say on those motivational websites. *Feelings, they are only feelings.* But just sitting with feelings can be the hardest task in the world.

Another thing: why do some people never catch fire? They never wake up. They are just content to look at you dully, even slack-jawed, when you make an important observation. Levels: it's as if it were all a matter of *levels of awareness*. And some people, for reasons that are not clear, are stuck at a certain level, mired in ignorance, inert, paralysed, even. Incompetent wasters, inadequates. They are a drain on the energy and insight of the others: that tiny number of awakened ones. Pray, read, withdraw, be silent, be at peace. And burn things.

———

Take great care not to splash any of the solvent on your fingers as you prepare the fire-lighter. Fluffy cotton wool makes the best "ground" for it. (Those mascara-remover discs are too thin and too absorbent; the flame doesn't take in the same way.) Use a screwdriver to lever up the lid of the modelmaker's tiny paint tin, these burn best in my experience. When you are confident that the cotton wool is sufficiently soaked in the paint, then strike a match and ignite it. There will be lots of white smoke. The smoke is how we sign our work.

History's greatest fire-starters, who were they? Certainly the Early Men must be counted among them, those proto-humans who roasted mammoths to death in a pit stacked with brushwood and timber for the purpose. Can we call Nero a fire-starter? Or did he only fiddle while Rome burned? The Nazis burned down the Reichstag and blamed an idiot-stooge. The Great Fire of London was not a deliberate fire but the Mayor refused to tear down the houses that would have stopped its spread, so that makes him a friend of the fire, in a manner of speaking, even if not a fully fledged fire-starter.

Then there were the bomber-pilots who destroyed Dresden. Hundreds of civilians huddling in cellars to avoid the suffocating firestorm that burned for days. And the Fascist pilots in Spain in 1937 who strafed and machine-gunned firemen fighting the flames in Barcelona and other Spanish cities. *Neeeeeee-oooowwmm*. *Buddahbuddahbuddah*. Look, there's one swaying at the top of a ladder with his fire-hose. Leave him to me. *Gottim*.

The history of men lighting fires is the true history of Man, a glorious saga of creation and destruction. Phoenixes rising from ashes forever and ever. Amen. I want my name to be inscribed in letters of flame in the roll-call of heroes in that Burning Book.

———

The Wychwode Inn, the Art Gallery in the village square and St Michael's - each of these poses a particular problem. (In addition to the problem that I like some of their occupants, that is.)

Take the Wychwode. They have a little dog in there, his name is Patchy, a Jack Russell terrier. You can throw a lime or a lemon and he will retrieve it, no matter how far it bounces into the dark interior of the pub. Patchy can jump so smartly onto a barstool from a standing start on the floor that you would swear that little dog is a master of levitation. Never seen anything like it. But his owner the publican of the Wychwode (whose name I refuse to give) is a bully. I can only hope that at the critical moment Patchy will not be locked up indoors.

Now as for the Art Gallery in the square opposite the church, that will have to go just because the so-called art on display inside is so bad. Nothing personal against the owners, but really. Those acrylics and watercolours are so anodyne as to be offensive. End of story.

St Michael's and All Angels and its clergy are

another special case. The priest has obviously lost his faith, if he ever had one. I have listened to too many of his lifeless sermons in that gloomy cold stone interior. I can almost hear the bonfire already consuming his church. But technically the church poses my toughest problem. Those heavyweight doors act as a complete fire brake and there is no other way in. Only a frontal assault to smash open those heavy ancient wooden doors stands any chance of success. There is no other access to the place. This will require some careful thought.

DC Isabel Archer was first on the scene at St Michael's during the serial arson attacks at the Cotswold village. She was only glad that no one had actually died in the fires (although one man was in intensive care). She was relieved too that her transfer from the Paedophile Unit had gone so smoothly. A case like this one was much more to her taste.

The vicar and his distraught wife and daughter made a forlorn spectacle huddled together and wailing at intervals in the village square.

Over at the Wychwode, the case was different. The Wychwode's publican was already in hospital. But his dog had escaped harm, evidently - the little Jack Russell was yapping excitedly at the police officer carrying it to a nearby police van.

One elderly witness - a lady in her late 70s who still taught the McTimony Technique and who looked much younger than her calendar age - had a fairly full description of the fire-starter. Ellen Varney, 77, described a man of early middle age in a white jumpsuit, black glasses and a vivid cherry crash hat, walking briskly and purposefully (but calmly and in no kind of a panic, she emphasised) away from the crime scene's crackling fires and percussive imploding windows.

Ms Varney had been out for a very early morning stroll around the village. On her way back she had passed the blazing church and the pub which was only then catching fire, smoke beginning to pour from the second-floor. (Residents across the street had by then already raised the alarm.)

It was after taking the vigorous senior lady's statement that DC Bryant caught sight of the CC camera at gutter-height on the front of the barbershop. She made a note to follow it up with the barbershop's owner.

Curtain-twitcher's account (as told to police):

The suspect was observed to leave his house soon after sunrise. He was wearing white overalls or a boiler suit and a red motorcycle crash helmet. He crossed the street to his adjacent garage and drove his secondhand BMW onto the road. Then he went back into his house and came out a few minutes later dragging a mattress. He stuffed this into the passenger side front-seat, shouldering the door shut after an arduous wrestling match with the bulky mattress. Then he walked around the front of the car and got into the driver's seat. Seated, he put on a pair of sunglasses. He drove off slowly, turning right at the end of the road, heading up Main Street towards the north end of the village.

———

Video camera footage from the Turkish Barbershop:

Note: Mr Kemal Ahmet installed a camera on the outside of his men's hair salon after several episodes in which his brand new Aston Martin was vandalised by local youths. The area of the car park on which he focused the lens of his security camera included much of the village square in its wider field (even though much of the footage is grainy and indistinct). The camera's angle from the Turkish Barbershop was a happy chance for the police investigators, one of whom had the bright idea of following up the lead at the crime scene once the square had been taped off by forensics.

The scruffy BMW roared across the square as if it had come from the direction of the Co-Op. It was heading straight for the doors that were the main entrance of St Michael and All Angels church, locked at this time of day. Just before impact, the crash-helmeted driver could be seen to throw himself sideways into the leg space of the passenger side. The hood of the car struck the heavy wooden doors with a deafening bang and a loud crack. Splinters of wood and fragments of glass from the shattered headlights exploded into the square. The car, still hurtling forward, disappeared into the entrance hallway of the church, followed a moment later by another loud bang as it struck an obstacle inside. Wisps of smoke began to issue from the splintered church doors hanging brokenly on their hinges, giving way after a few minutes to huge billows of white smoke. Flames illuminated the stained glass of the church windows, quickly building to something approaching an inferno.

A white boiler-suited figure in dark glasses and red crash helmet sprinted out of the church, heading for the nearby village Art Gallery about a hundred yards away. The figure is off-camera for about five minutes before it is seen running again - away from the Art Gallery - towards the Wychwode Inn pub on the opposite side of the square.

The figure is next seen to crouch down by the door of the main entrance and to manipulate the letterbox for a minute or two. (The details are hazy at this range, the camera working at the limits of its performance.) After a few minutes, an upstairs window is smashed from the inside the pub and smoke issues from it. A shouting commotion starts up inside.

The boiler-suited figure turns on his heel and walks briskly out of range.

The whole village is still in shock as I write. There are news items six pages deep on Google. And that amateurish local newsletter website Wychwode Update is full of it! A great carpet of fire, that's what it must have looked like from the air. Like a burning ordnance-survey map, contours blurring in a blizzard of sparks, of smoke. The wings of a great bird carried me off, away to Berlin, from where I write, sitting in a trendy cafe. I have made my demonstration. They said I was some sort of mentalist. But now they have a better estimate of my vision, my powers.

The End

ACCIDENT ON A SUBURBAN DRIVE

JACK D MCLEAN

When I got together with Gerald, a formula as old as our species was at work.

He was forty-one, I was twenty-five; he was rich and I was poor. He looked just about okay from a distance whereas I was, and still am, quite stunning. That's not just my opinion. People tell me that all the time, and not just my Mum and Dad.

Gerald gave me a home and security and in return I brought glamour into his life. Heads turned and jaws dropped when we were out and about together – he loved that.

I was his trophy girlfriend who provided sex on tap even when I didn't feel like it, and conversation if required. I didn't do any housework, though. That wasn't part of the deal. No way.

The sixteen-year age gap wasn't excessive in my opinion. I've seen bigger in the Sugar Babe community. There were drawbacks of course. I expected that.

For instance, some of those heads that turned, you could tell the owners of them were thinking:

What's she doing with him?

But when we got into his chauffeur-driven Bentley Mulsanne at the end of the evening it was obvious what I was doing with him. And most eyes that looked on us were the darkest of bottle green with envy.

Then there was his body. I've had sex with men my own age and they had nice firm bodies, at least, the ones who looked after themselves did. I'm afraid Gerald didn't.

Unsurprisingly, given who he was having sex with, a part of him could always be relied upon to be firm. But the rest of him was soft and flabby. At least he didn't have man-boobs, thank God. I don't think I could've coped with that.

He smoked, drank heavily, and the hardest exercise he ever took was rumpy-pumpy with me on the kitchen table. He hurt his knee getting on it, so after that we only ever did it in his bed.

He was very unhealthy my Gerald. Still, I never expected he'd die so young, just four years after we got together, aged only forty-five. It wasn't his health that killed him. He had an accident. If not for that we might still be together. I like to think so.

He ate all the wrong things so it wasn't surprising that he was overweight. What was surprising was that he was clinically obese. That's what the doctor said, anyway. But he hid it well under his tailored jackets and thick sweaters. You'd never have guessed that Gerald was clinically obese.

You'd just have classed him as stocky.

Well, he was a bit on the short side. He was five

feet four my Gerald. I'm five foot five and in my heels I'm more like five-ten. I used to tower over him. He had to stand on his tippy-toes to kiss me. That was all to the good, really. He used to find it exciting, dating a woman who was bigger than him. Which was fortunate, because every woman he was likely to meet would give him a run for his money in the height department, especially with heels on.

He was my investment for the future, my pension. I always thought I'd marry Gerald and we'd settle down, have children, but we never did. I lived with him in his mansion and enjoyed all the benefits of a sugar-daddy – a car, roof over my head, and more pocket-money than the average person gets paid in this country, but we never got hitched.

I call it pocket-money but I actually had a job-title. Personal assistant. It was a tax-wheeze of some kind. I can assure you that the only assistance I ever gave Gerald was of the most personal kind you can get.

It all went swimmingly for a few years but things started to go wrong when I mentioned marriage.

"We've been together a while now, Gerald," I said one summer day out in the garden.

He was on the croquet lawn practising some shots; I was watching him with a gin and tonic in my hand.

"What's that Amanda?" He said, looking up from the ball.

"We've been together a while now," I repeated. "It's about time you made an honest woman of me."

He struck the ball with a crack and it shot through a little wooden arch a few feet away.

"An honest woman, eh? I'm not sure I'm ready for

that. Can't we just go on the way we are? We're both happy, aren't we?"

"Well, yes, but ..."

"Then why fix it, if it ain't broke?"

"But, because, well ... "

There was a noise like Tarzan calling in the jungle. He took his mobile phone from his pocket. Gerald could be very childish in some ways. He put the phone to his ear.

"Yes, yes," he said. Then he looked at me. "Business. You'll have to excuse me for a while."

I sloped indoors and topped up my gin.

Over the next few months we had a lot of conversations such as:

"We've been together nearly four years now, Gerald. The clock's ticking. I want children. What are you going to do about it?"

"Can we discuss this some other time please, Amanda? I have these accounts to look at right now."

Somehow he always seemed to wriggle out of giving me the commitment I needed.

Then one day I decided to have it out with him once and for all.

"I'm sick of waiting for you Gerald. Can't you see that?"

"Waiting for me?"

"Waiting for you to make up your mind. As far as I can see, this relationship isn't going anywhere."

"Where do you want it to go?"

"Into a church then on to a honeymoon somewhere exotic."

"Oh, er ..." There was a Tarzan call, as there always seemed to be at awkward moments like this one. "Business," he said. "Please excuse me."

It made me wonder if he'd had some special thing going to make his phone go off at will to end our conversations when they were getting difficult for him.

One day he left his mobile lying around. So I picked it up to check if there was any way he could be making it go off at will like that.

And when I did, I saw a text. To a girl. Called Felicity.

"Dear Felicity, can't wait to meet up tomorrow, love and kisses xxx",

When I looked closer there was a whole chain of text messages between him and this floozy and they sent love and kisses to each other in every single fucking one of them. She'd sent pictures of herself, the little whore. In some of them she was on holiday in a bikini.

It seemed I had a rival for Gerald's affections. He'd cheated on me. My blood, of course, boiled.

How long had this been going on? What did she mean to him, this Felicity?

Obviously, marriage was out of the question, now. I have my pride. I wasn't going to marry Gerald knowing he was seeing another woman behind my back.

I packed my bags and threw them in the back of my car, a VW Golf convertible. The roof was down as it was a sunny day.

Turning on the ignition I saw Gerald in the rear-view mirror, emerging from the house. He called after me.

"You didn't say you were going out!"

"I'm not," I screeched without even turning my head. "I'm leaving you!"

He started walking towards my car.

"Leaving me? I don't understand. Why?"

"You know full well why!"

My car was an automatic. I slipped it into drive.

"No, I don't!"

"It's that floozy you've been seeing behind my back?"

"Floozy?"

"You can't even be honest with me, can you?"

My blood pressure soared, I got a sort of red mist before my eyes and before I knew what I was doing I'd put the car into reverse, released the handbrake, and stepped on the gas.

Within a second I'd mown him down.

Then panic set in. I drove forward until I was sure the car wasn't on top of him and got out. He looked very dead and as far as I could tell, looks didn't deceive. I dialled 999.

"There's been a terrible accident. I need an ambulance."

"What is the address, madam?"

I told them where I was.

"Please describe the accident."

"I ran over my boyfriend by mistake."

"And how is he?"

"He appears to be dead."

"An ambulance is on its way."

When the ambulance arrived it was accompanied by a police car. The paramedics confirmed Gerald was dead and I burst into tears. When the police asked me about it I said:

"I was in a bit of a tizzy and I put the car into reverse instead of drive by mistake."

Then I looked at them with puppy-dog eyes, and thank heavens they believed me.

Gerald's parents organised his funeral. They were distraught, poor things, but they managed.

Afterwards at the funeral meal a young woman came up to me. I recognised her at once. Felicity. I determined not to bring up the matter of Gerald cheating on me with her. Didn't want to cause a scene, not at his funeral.

"You're Amanda, aren't you?" She asked.

"Yes," I said, wondering where she was going with the conversation and why we were even talking.

"I don't believe he told you about me."

"No, he didn't."

"I'm his daughter."

"His daughter?"

"Yes. I feel almost as if I know you because he used to talk about you all the time. I always hoped we'd get to meet, but not in circumstances like this, obviously. Perhaps I should explain that I only knew Gerald for a brief period. You see, he didn't know he had a daughter until I made a point of getting in touch with him three months ago. My mother never told him she was pregnant with his child when they split up. Anyway, it was traumatic for us both, getting to know each other. He told me he didn't want us to come out, as it were, as father and daughter, until he'd got used to the idea. I think he was on the verge of telling everyone about me, but tragically his accident stopped him from doing that."

I poured myself a large glass of Chardonnay and gulped it down in one.

The End

MILLENNIUM BRIDGE CONVERSATIONS

MARTIN MULLIGAN

It's no surprise that China sells the best listening devices in the world today, sound-guns for spies. (Texas comes in a close second.) What is surprising is how much these electronic ears can catch, even a quarter of a mile away from, say, a wind-whipped steel bridge, its rigging singing as it resonates to a storm sweeping up the Thames Estuary. But I'm getting ahead of myself already. Bear with me a moment.

I'm a writer, you see, and I had a winning idea for a book. It would be made up of captured clandestine conversations, overheard at all seasons and times of day. Every conversation would have in common with the others only this: each exchange in the book would have taken place - secretly overheard - on London's celebrated Millennium Bridge, which links Sam Wanamaker's restored Shakespeare's Globe with St Paul's Cathedral. That iconic walkway hums and strums and trembles like a violin string in all weathers.

These stolen conversations, about which the original participants would never learn, would act as the starting point for stories in an award-winning collection. That, at least, was my plan.

Now, always to separate planning from execution is a first principle of management and it served me well in this case. Because the first part of my plan went swimmingly.

All I did was to order the sound-gun (to be exact: the Parabolic Catch-all Electronic Microphone Spy Listening Device) from a dealer in Shenzhen via the global marketplace. A couple of clicks on the website of the digital dealer that is a household name worldwide and within a week a package was on my doorstep. I unwrapped the dinky little parcel like a kid at Christmas, eyes wide at the splendid Sputnik-era ray-gun design.

On my first trial-run of it in my neighbourhood I picked up a lively domestic argument in a three-bedroom semi, simply by pointing it at an upstairs window from the cover of a forsythia bush at the street corner. Those expletives and shouted threats followed by tears were all crystal-clear, the reception was brilliant.

Little wonder then that I could hardly wait to get the train to London and Shakespeare's Bankside in order to set up my spy-hide close to the Millennium Bridge. I was straining at the leash to start the R&D for my big writing project. Man Booker Prize nominations, cafe-chain sponsorships, national followed by international author tours, my head was spinning with every last detail of the book racket's glamour and glare before I'd written even a word. But that's all part of the writer's psyche, I told myself. It's the sheer glory of the thing that pulls us forward.

Never point a sound-gun directly at a blackhead gull. The squawk that creature can generate is an ear-bursting phenomenon even without an amplifier. You would think blood was running from your eyes afterwards, I'm not kidding. There were lots of seabirds about that day, maybe a storm at sea had driven them inland. The sound-gun and headphones took a bit of setting up in the lee of the gale blowing up the Thames estuary. It was mainly a question of being fairly well-concealed, as well as having a clear field for the device to listen at a distance.

I had the range pretty much right now (after a false step or two, such as picking out that seagull perched on the handrail). People were moving back and forth on the bridge in the late afternoon. They were mainly individuals in suits walking determinedly on their way to God knows what self-important business assignations in coffee shops or boardrooms (meetings, meetings, the very lifeblood of conformist managerial capitalism). Black overcoats and well-cut charcoal grey suits, black briefcases, shiny black shoes, all flowing steadily across the Millennium Bridge. A steady procession of dyed dark hair and once-handsome faces now strained and pallid or chubby and florid.

I had gotten used to this slow-motion tide of metropolitan types when I was brought up short by two figures walking towards the St Paul's side of the bridge, against the flow of the office crowd.

They were two scruffy, ill-matched characters: a tall, rangy fellow in a black leather jacket and sunglasses and a smaller, nimble, nervous-looking young man with darting eyes, wearing a hoodie with a cartoon-shark surfing logo on it. Each stood out glaringly in this heartland of sartorial conformity.

They halted in the middle of the bridge, standing side-by-side against the handrail, facing Southwark Bridge half-a-mile away downstream. Their positioning was perfect in terms of line of sight and a direct auditory bearing for my sound-gun. It was all almost too good to be true for my purposes.

Of course, I could not know then that one of them was not only a thief but also a sadistic homicidal maniac.

———

Back home in Wychwode later that day I was transcribing the tape I'd made of the several conversations I'd captured on the bridge. Most were quite anodyne exchanges about restaurants, public transport hassles and office gossip. Then I zeroed in on the conversation between the two unkempt types I'd aimed the gun at, the pair talking (furtively, it seemed) in the middle of the bridge, as if they had especially not wanted to be overheard. I read and reread the transcript. Then I returned to the tape recording to check, twice. Still it beggared belief. I went back to listen to it from beginning to end for a third time.

They were planning to turn over an entire apartment block in Kensington. Nine apartments during the course of a holiday weekend. They had even let slip the address of the place. It had a concierge and a full-time security guard. I could not believe what I was hearing. "We shut down all communications." The tall, wolf-like type was speaking. "Half the rich bastards will be away at their holiday cottages or second homes. We take our whole crew and we take our time, half the night if needs be. Room by room, however long it takes. No rush about any of it once we've taken care of their security. Then we fill both vans with the stuff and just drive away."

Most people would take this to the police immediately. But I couldn't. The reasons why are not important. Let's just say I'd had too many scrapes just this side of the law for too many years and my name was already a familiar one in police circles, not in a good way. I'd been acquitted twice. One time I went surety in a Home Office case for a Ukrainian asylum-seeker, a gay physics teacher beaten up and driven from his own country, who'd eventually won the right to stay. The authorities had not liked it. So I was reluctant, to say the least, to trouble them with this latest development.

Besides, how was I going to justify my blatant invasion of rights of privacy by my sound-gun exploits, in the first place? "Oh yes, officer, that. Well, it was going to be the starting point for a book, you see, officer." No, I couldn't see how I could possibly pitch up at the police reception desk with that as a justification.

———

Which explains how I came to be standing in a doorway opposite 113 Sitwell Mansions on a cold, indeed a very cold, let's face it a frankly freezing February morning. My breath formed feathers of ice, I was stamping my feet in a futile bid to keep warm.

I'd been watching the place at intervals since I'd stumbled across the planned heist, hoping for some hint or clue that would give me a handle somehow to intervene safely. I had a bad feeling about the whole thing and was convinced that innocents would be hurt unless something was done. (Even rich innocents deserve a fighting chance, after all.) For all I knew, some of the targets of the robbery might even have children at home that weekend. No doubt about it, this thing had to be prevented somehow, even if it put me in the line of fire.

During the four days running up to the holiday weekend nothing suspicious had happened that I could make out. (There was a false alarm on Wednesday when I thought I recognised the guy dropping off a package at reception. It turned out to be only a courier with some dry-cleaning on hangers all meticulously bagged up in polythene.)

On Friday, out of patience, I decided desperate measures were called for.

I crossed the street from my still chilly vantage

point, strode into the lobby of the apartment block past the well-kept rubber plants and straight up to the imposing teak counter behind which a pale-blue uniformed concierge was lounging in a chair on wheels (reading, I noticed, The Sun). He was a big man, his lantern-jaw unshaven. He wore a peaked cap with a brass shield-badge on the front of it. He looked like nothing so much as a wannabe New York Police Department extra with an obesity issue. Never mind all that, I thought. My plan was to say my bit and then to leave at once.

I placed my hands on the counter and leaned forward to emphasise the gravity of my mission. Without pausing to introduce myself, I said: "Look, pal, I'm not going to dress this up. Your place is the target of gang of thieves this weekend. You'd do well to call the cops right now and get the place covered. I'm not taking questions about this. Thanks, bye." Then I looked quickly, interrogatively, deep into his small button-like porcine eyes - pale blue, I saw, like the uniform - to be sure he had got the message. I was poised to lean back, to turn on my heel and stride out.

What happened next surprised me. He leapt up, sending his chair on casters flying backwards. There was a blur in my left field of vision. Then discontinuity.

The blur was his fist the size of a frozen leg of lamb. The discontinuity was it striking my head.

There's a B-movie cliche that someone who has been knocked out sees the faces of three people occupying his field of vision. The soundtrack runs: "He's coming round, he's coming round." (With a booing echo-chamber timbre.) Except that it's not only a cinematic cliche. That is also what happens sometimes in so-called real life.

The three faces in my wavering vision were those of the hulking concierge, the lupine character I'd seen on the bridge and his slighter, jumpy associate. I felt 40-feet tall and one-inch wide, with a head made of stale candy-floss. A giant squid of a headache had its blood-funnel rammed between my eyebrows. I could not trust myself to open my eyes for long, let alone to say anything. A jagged bit of tooth was snagging sharply against my tongue and the inside of my cheek on the right side. I spat out very feebly a fragment of broken tooth and felt a bloody drool crawl down my chin, as if I was at the dentist.

"Spider, you've got to see this, it changes everything," the nervous thin young man was saying in an East European accent.

"No, it doesn't. It changes nothing. We're still on." The evil-looking tall rangy one, with limbs like steel levers (a fascist body-type if ever I saw one) was wearing the distressed black leather jacket he'd had on that day at the bridge.

"What if he's already gone to the law? We don't know if he may have grassed us up."

"Relax, will you. I'll find out what he knows soon enough. And we are still on. No worries, this little development isn't a deal breaker. Don't let on to the rest of the crew. Make sure those alley doors are open for loading at midnight."

I had lost all track of time but reckoned now that I can't have been unconscious for much more than a few minutes. Just long enough for them to drag me out of sight across the lobby to a store room. But I felt too weak even to talk or to protest. So I just lay there, quietly bleeding on the floor of the janitor's cupboard, it looked like, among the mops and cleaning fluids in their hard plastic containers. Although I was spitting blood and moaning softly, the ammoniac odours were helping a little, like smelling salts in a boxer's corner between rounds.

I heard the door close, a sign that two of the (quite literal) partners in crime had left me and the menacing Spider alone. Plainly but coldly furious, he quickly proceeded to make my life even more of a misery. On the plus side, I passed out again when he started to belabour my midsection with his Doc Martens.

He eventually left me tied with wire to a shelf, with my feet barely touching the floor. By that time I had bruises on my chest and ribs that were so painful I wondered if a rib had gone but as my breathing was still OK I guessed not. My right eye was completely closed and my left one nearly so. The broken tooth hurt like hell and I was having trouble feeling my fingertips. My lips and nose were streaming blood from the secondary bashing Spider had administered over my blubbering insistence that I had told nobody about what I'd learned on the bridge. At last he'd seemed satisfied enough to quit the cupboard and to leave me quietly bleeding and gagged. Gagged with a rag that smelled of turpentine. At least that's what I told myself when I became gradually conscious again in the dark of the janitor's storeroom.

I'd been in that condition for an hour, I would estimate (my time-perception was coming and going), when the door opened a tiny crack and light angled across the floor from the well-lit lobby. There was a pause and then the door opened fully and closed quickly with a deft click behind a figure ducking hurriedly into my cupboard of pain. Then we were in the near-dark again.

It was the anxious young man. He wasted no time in talk and was already fumbling with the wire that Spider had lashed around my wrists. From his haste and his stertorous shallow breathing, very loud in our confined space, I guessed he still had scruples about the whole plan. But what with the gag in my mouth, and one thing and another, I could hardly ask him. There was an intermittent ringing in my ears now as well that had me worried. My head after all had taken some punishment. Anyway he was shushing me desperately to stay silent as he abandoned the wire on my wrists - it had proved too stubborn - and tore at the wire knots that were cutting into my shins. I was still suspended from a high shelf by the wire around my wrists, looking like a Poundland Saint Sebastian.

After several minutes of this fevered broddling about in the gloom of the janitor's store-cupboard, my feet and legs were free. But as he went back to work on my hands and wrists (now completely numb) , a sudden racket could be heard from the lobby through the closed door: "Stoyan! Where the fuck are you?".

My would-be rescuer froze. He abandoned his bid to free my hands. I started to mumble through the turpentine gag but he clamped a surprisingly strong hand over my mouth. Then the pressure on my gag eased, the door again opened (a slender momentary cone of light) and he was gone.

More shouting from the lobby. Running footsteps and sounds of pursuit, then nothing. Four or five minutes or so later, I swear I heard brakes and tyres shrieking from a way off - but it could have been an auditory hallucination. I'd taken a hammering and was still literally seeing stars. My head had become unreliable. Everything seemed painful. But I began to move my legs about as best I could, trying to restore the circulation. Also in order to be ready for a final desperate effort to defend myself if Spider came back.

Let's be clear, I had no choice. It's not as if the guy had a better nature to which I could appeal. He had amply demonstrated that. The steadily pooling blood - my blood, remember - that was drip-drip-dripping onto the shelves and floor of the janitor's cupboard was a vivid reminder. I'm no hero and I'd been singing like a canary (which was once a startling simile) about the bridge and how I knew about their plans even before Spider started to kick lumps out of me. But a cornered man tied by wire in a cupboard has very little left to lose.

Spider did come back, of course he did. That maniac could not stop himself.

It happened like this. I had just come round from another fitful daze, still bleeding from my mouth and wrists. (Would it never end?) The floor was by now positively slippery. I felt too weak and watery for what I had to do.

Spider snapped on the light and advanced towards me, snarling and swearing. And this time with a crowbar, I happened to notice, dangling from his left hand. His right was balled into a fist and about to strike my undefended head again.

Now, I hadn't wasted the time and opportunity afforded by those untied feet and shins before the one called Stoyan lost his nerve, gave up his attempt to free me, and legged it out of my gloomy cupboard of horror.

In fact I'd managed very painfully to drag a heavy vulcanised rubber mop-bucket to me in the dark. Into this I had plunged my right foot and lower leg, as if into a giant's ugly boot lifted from a tale by the Brothers Grimm. My foot was firmly rammed and jammed in there. Never mind the protests of my shins, my life was riding on this.

With a lupine smile now animating his pale and pockmarked face, his right fist still cocked, taking his time, Spider was planting his feet wide and settling into a Kung fu horse-stance, the better to give me an epic beating.

I yelled and lashed upwards with the bucket-weapon firmly affixed to my foot, bracing on the floor as best I could with my left leg to get some proper purchase to leverage the blow. I was blessed with good luck. It caught the startled Spider full in the crotch.

I heard his reflex intake of breath as the blinding pain hit.

I had to exploit this brief, this very brief, moment of advantage or it was all over for me. The pain from my wrists which were taking my full weight and dragging on the shelf was excruciating. All that would have to wait. Spider stood rigid in shock and I kicked him again, with my left leg this time, in the same place; a perfect penalty kick to his unprotected groin.

The crowbar fell with a metallic tink! to the cement floor next to some canisters of bleach.

He hissed and fell to his knees, then tilted forward on all fours, parallel to the floor that was slick with my blood. His head and shoulders were at my feet. The gods were still smiling on me.

I caught Spider's jaw a clumsy glancing kick with the heel of my free foot. It was a weak blow and it nearly missed but it was enough. As his face went to the floor, I brought the vulcanised rubber boot awkwardly but solidly down on the back of his head. And again. I kept this up until he stopped moving. Then, gibbering and weeping in terror, in a final frenzy, I did it some more. (He had tried to kill me, you understand.)

After that there was a time when I sort of lost track of things in my bloody cupboard, still wire-tied by the wrists in an enclosed space with a homicidal maniac whose breathing I could no longer hear.

My shins and the arch of my right foot were protesting with an ache that was hard to bear. I wondered again if I'd broken something there to go with my red hot needle-pierced ribs and wrists. It helped that I kept blacking out. Everything was surreal now in my cosy warm Doctor Caligari's cabinet. I was talking and giggling to myself at intervals there in that cupboard, I noticed. I could hear it. But it was so faint and broken-up, like snatches of birdsong in a darkling wood as night falls, that only a sound-gun could have made it out.

Two people died that night. The first was the young man called Stoyan who had tried to set me free before his psycho associate came back to finish me off.

When Spider rumbled him he fled into the street and kept running in his panic and got himself run over by an ambulance. That was the siren and the street sounds I thought I'd heard. Police showed up soon afterwards. I learned much later that Stoyan, conscious but with not long to live, stammered something on the pavement or on a stretcher that led them to Sitwell Mansions. (Was he having a panic attack and/or crisis of conscience? Had he helped me because he knew of Spider's murderous nature and intentions?)

If you ask me I probably saved a cop's life by taking the action I did against Spider. Because you will have guessed already that his was the other corpse. Fighting for my life in that blacked-out storeroom, my frenzied lashing out in self-defence had quite done for Spider, it turned out.

Judge and jury were lenient when the full facts were laid before them. I got a four-year custodial. That's how I came to be writing this, the title story of Millennium Bridge Conversations, in the library of Ford Open Prison during my final stretch. Wondering now about making at least the Man Booker long-list.

PHOEBE

JACK D MCLEAN

The young woman swivelled her eyes desperately to avoid my own. She must have known I'd been watching her but she had no idea why. Probably she thought I fancied her. It wasn't as simple as that.

Undoubtedly she was the sort of woman any straight man would find attractive but that wasn't why I was interested in her. It was something to do with the way she carried herself.

I was so impressed by the woman's posture and movements that I used my mobile to make a short video of her. It may have been this that sparked the incident. I wasn't being in any way provocative; I was trying to catch the essence of what made her a woman. But I was misunderstood. I have often been misunderstood.

After taking the video I began making notes in the spiral bound notepad I carry around for use in situations such as this. I became so engrossed in my work that I didn't notice the brawny young man she was with detach himself from her group and walk over to where I was sitting.

I was in a side booth on my own. It is a habit of mine to take up solitary vantage points so that I can observe women in their natural habitat going about their business.

I didn't become aware of the young man until I felt his hand on my shoulder and looked up. He thrust his face close to mine. Even in the gloom of the bar I could see that his skin was coarse and unpleasant.

"Listen Granddad," he snarled. He was so close to me that I felt the warmth of his stinking breath on my face. "My friend's fucking sick of you perving all over her. I'd punch yer fucking lights out if you weren't such a fucking useless old git. Now fuck off out of here before I change my mind and assault a pensioner."

He had it all wrong. I hadn't been perving at all. I had been gathering material.

I felt two emotions in equal measure: fear and anger. I was angry enough to smack him one, but fear of the consequences held me back. He was thickset and looked as if he could take care of himself. That did not bode well. I am thickset too, but only around the middle. The rest of my frame is skinny. My shoulders are narrow and my arms are feeble pipe stems.

Thrusting my notebook and pen into my pocket, I stood up hurriedly. I was all too aware that my legs were trembling uncontrollably. They felt as if they might buckle under my weight.

I am 50 years old and no granddad, considering myself virile. But there was no point in explaining any of this to the young thug who was on the verge of assaulting me. Leaving with as much dignity as I could muster, I felt the glare of multiple pairs of eyes boring into my back.

It was something of a shock to emerge from the darkness of the bar into bright afternoon sunshine. I blinked a few times before my eyes became accustomed to the new lighting conditions. It was Friday afternoon and Manchester's Northern Quarter was bustling. I caught sight of a woman who would normally have aroused my interest, but I was still in a state of shock because of what had happened in the Black Dog Bar, so I ignored her. Instead I headed straight for my car and drove to my studio.

My studio is in a terraced house in Withington, once an attractive village but now absorbed into the urban sprawl of Greater Manchester. Going inside, I hurried up to the attic away from prying eyes, downloaded my latest video onto my pc, and saved it in a file I had prepared many months before called "Manchester Girls – Northern Quarter".

I played it over and over again, carefully observing the way that my new starlet sashayed confidently across the polished floor of the Black Dog. It was serious research.

Afterwards I undressed and delved into the chest of drawers I keep in the attic then put on a pair of the women's knickers I conceal there. I could have managed without them of course. After all, my underwear wouldn't be seen and there was no one around to judge me. I wasn't going to venture out in public. But I would judge myself and I would know that the creature I was creating wouldn't be authentic if I didn't wear the knickers. Every last detail had to be perfect otherwise I wouldn't be satisfied.

I put on my corset. It does a good job of holding in my belly and it imparts the hint of a woman's curves to my hips. Next came my falsies and bra. Then the dress.

At that stage I glanced at myself in one of the many full-length mirrors I keep in the attic. I looked like a middle-aged man in a woman's clothing.

To complete the transformation I was after, I donned a wig and carefully applied makeup to my face. Then I looked in the mirror again. I was no beauty but I had at least become a woman, or something that resembled a woman.

Now you may think I am gay or a transvestite or a wannabe transsexual. I can assure you that I am none of these things. I am an artist pure and simple.

Well, I was once pure and I was once simple. But that was a long time ago. I have lost my purity and my naivety forever. My wife and her lover have seen to that.

I walked gracefully back and forth like the woman I had become, aping as best I could the sashaying motion of the woman I had seen in the Black Dog. Every now and again I checked my form in one of my mirrors to make sure I was getting it right. And for the most part I was. It was an accomplished Performance. But it was not good enough for me. My creation did not please me. I had known all along that it would be inadequate; it always was.

It was with sadness that I removed my dress, undergarments, and makeup, and resumed my usual identity: Herbert Bottomley, Herb to his friends, the local minor artist.

Minor Artist. *Minor*. How I longed to be a *Major* Artist. One of the Britpack. Another Damien Hirst, say, or (perhaps more appropriately) a Tracey Emin.

Not that I was doing so badly. I was making a living from my work and a fair living at that, which is more than most modern artists can say. My problem was that it was a living based on types of art which held no interest for me.

I had a steady stream of clients wanting me to make portraits of them. The rest of my paid work came from restoration and the like. But I was longing to make money from my original work. It mattered to me. But all it seemed to do was make the place untidy. It didn't sell, and it didn't bring in any money.

———

After I had cleaned every last scrap of makeup from my face I went downstairs and worked on a half-finished sculpture bringing it a step nearer to completion. My concentration was such that I didn't notice the passage of time. Before I knew it Friday had become Saturday and it was nearly 1.00 a.m. so I locked up my studio and went home. Home is another terraced house in Withington which I share with my wife Cleo.

———

Latex, that was the answer.

As soon as the idea occurred to me I wondered why I hadn't thought of it before.

Simply put, I could make my ideal woman out of latex and wear her like a suit. My sagging face would no longer be the limiting factor on my appearance, nor would my less than ample hips. Latex could give me the shape and facial features of the woman of my dreams.

No sooner did the idea occur to me than I set to work feverishly to accomplish my goal. Luckily I was no stranger to the medium. I'd had a great deal of experience of working with latex as an art student and more recently on a rather exotic commission.

I made a bust of the ideal woman's head and shoulders, taking care to ensure that it was slightly larger than my own. I used the bust to make a casting with plastic eyes. A body soon followed, then arms and legs.

I worked night and day on my project. I don't think Cleo missed me during this period. Doubtless she was too busy fucking Max, or thinking about fucking him, when she was not actually fucking him.

The exciting day came when everything was ready. Stripping naked I prepared myself with liberal quantities of talcum powder.

Taking the body which was something like a leotard I stepped into it, easing it up to my neck. The breasts were spectacular if somewhat immobile.

Next I poured talcum powder into the latex legs and carefully pulled them over my own legs. They instantly transformed my knobbly specimens into pins that would have done justice to a lingerie model. Latex sleeves performed a similar service for my arms.

Finally came the crowning masterpiece. The head. I lowered it over my own and tightened the laces at the back. A flowing wig of black hair topped it off.

When I looked around the attic the visibility I had through the cunningly engineered eyes was surprisingly good. When I caught sight of my reflection it amazed me. I had at last created a woman. The most beautiful woman I have ever seen.

Turning this way and that I admired myself – *herself* – in the mirror. My God, she was beautiful My God, *I* was beautiful.

Studying my high cheekbones, my full lips, my breasts, my pubic hair and my long legs, I came to the conclusion that they were all perfect.

I stepped up close to the mirror. It was only when I was up very close that my face took on a slightly doll-like appearance. If anything it was an improvement on real life. It is after all a compliment to refer to a woman as a living doll.

The sight of my own nakedness began to arouse and embarrass me in equal measure. My face reddened beneath the latex that covered it. Soon I realised why. It was not me who was embarrassed. It was my creation. She did not appreciate being stared at while she was naked. In the interests of modesty, I, that is, she, donned a swimsuit — a skimpy yellow two-piece — and, suitably clothed, she allowed me to admire her. It was love at first sight.

I decided there and then to call her Phoebe. The shining one.

When I had first conceived of Phoebe I had thought only of her appearance and movements. I had given no consideration to her mind. She was to be little more than a marionette.

It took me by surprise that she would develop thoughts of her own. But that is exactly what she did.

———

In some ways Phoebe was like my mother who was a spiteful, vindictive woman; and treacherous and disloyal.

Little wonder my father committed suicide.

Notwithstanding her character defects, my mother was very beautiful and could be charming, at least in her youth.

Phoebe was unlike my mother in her treatment of me. She would never be disloyal to me and if she showed any hint of my mother's vindictiveness, it was others who would feel the sting of it, not her creator.

When I told Phoebe about the incident in The Black Dog, she was incensed. She told me to find out where the miscreant who had threatened me lived.

I spent all my spare time over the next couple of weeks hanging around outside the Black Dog. Eventually I was rewarded by the sight of the young man who had threatened me leaving the place in an advanced a state of inebriation. He went to the cab rank in Piccadilly, got into a black cab, and set off to his destination. Climbing into the a cab just behind his I used the immortal words:

"Follow that car."

We twisted and turned on highway and by-way until eventually his cab pulled up outside a house on Claremont Road in Moss-Side. I told my driver to go straight past and I took a note of the house number.

As the young thug fumbled with his keys I reclined back in my seat, enjoying the prospect of telling Phoebe that I had tracked down my tormentor to his lair.

She wasted no time in righting the wrong that had been done to me.

After first arming herself with a kitchen knife she drove my car to Moss-Side and parked around the corner from Claremont Road. She got out of the car and walked briskly to Young Thug's house. Along the way she passed one or two people in the street walking their dogs and attracted glances, all of them admiring, no doubt. Her strange beauty is enough to turn anyone's head.

She knocked loudly on the door.

Young Thug opened it.

His reddened pock-marked features and foul breath were every bit as repellent to Phoebe as they had been to me.

She quickly produced the kitchen knife from her handbag and pushed the sharp tip up against his fat belly which was straining against the fabric of his white T-shirt.

He took a step back in horror. I knew why.

Phoebe's face was beautiful, doll-like, and entirely without pity.

Phoebe entered the gloomy hallway of his house pulling the door shut behind her.

Then, in an instant, she plunged the knife into his loathsome fat belly. When it was in deep she drew the blade sideways spilling his fat guts. They landed with an audible splash on the tiled floor.

He dropped into a sitting position and looked up at her.

"Why?" He said.

Phoebe's answer was brief and to the point: she slit his throat.

Then she left as quickly as she had arrived, the young thug now no more than a ghastly mess on a tiled floor which some unlucky person would have the unenviable task of cleaning up.

As Phoebe got into her car a woman passed by with her young son. She glanced in Phoebe's direction once then gave Phoebe a second, furtive, look. No doubt this was because an exotic beauty like Phoebe was a most unexpected sight in Moss Side. The woman must have been in a hurry to get somewhere because she grabbed her boy's hand and broke into a run, dragging him along with her until they were both out of sight.

When Phoebe got home she told me all about her exploits.

To be honest with you, I felt she'd gone a little bit too far. Still, I could forgive her any excess as I was by then madly in love with her.

To me she was the ideal woman.

This begs the question of what the ideal woman is. I had not previously given it much thought. But Phoebe made me consider the issue.

The ideal woman is one who is beautiful and will go to any lengths to protect her man.

She has asked me for a list of my enemies. I'm drawing one up right now.

Max is at the top of the list.

Cleo is just below him.

And there are quite a few others below Cleo.

When you are an artist you make enemies, I'm afraid. It goes with the territory.

The End

Dear reader,

We hope you enjoyed reading *Dirty Noir*. Please take a moment to leave a review, even if it's a short one. Your opinion is important to us.

Discover more books by Martin Mulligan at https://www.nextchapter.pub/authors/martin-mulligan

Want to know when one of our books is free or discounted? Join the newsletter at http://eepurl.com/bqqB3H

Best regards,

Martin Mulligan, Jack D McLean, and the Next Chapter Team

ABOUT THE AUTHOR
JACK D MCLEAN

The mysterious Jack D McLean hails from the town of Huddersfield, in West Yorkshire , England. He's a man with a checkered past, having worked in a morgue, been a labourer, and a salesman.

He's dug holes... *professionally* (to what end, he refuses to say – sales? corpses? possibly both?), even more terrifying – he's a former Lawyer. He enjoys parties and keeps himself fit (the kind of fit that makes you think he may engage in fisticuffs with Vinnie Jones on a semi-regular basis, or possibly drink stout with both hands while also throwing a perfect game of darts.) He is allegedly married with two adult daughters. They have yet to be located for comment.

ABOUT THE AUTHOR
MARTIN MULLIGAN

Martin Mulligan is a writer living in Oxford. He attended Lancaster University. He has written chiefly for the Financial Times, news and features. He spent a year in Beijing teaching journalism at Xinhua University and has travelled widely in Eastern Europe, Africa and south-east Asia. He is a keen open water swimmer.

Dirty Noir
ISBN: 978-4-82410-331-4
Mass Market

Published by
Next Chapter
1-60-20 Minami-Otsuka
170-0005 Toshima-Ku, Tokyo
+818035793528

6th September 2021